WALT DISNEY'S
Peter Pan and Wendy

TOLD BY ANNIE NORTH BEDFORD
ILLUSTRATIONS BY THE WALT DISNEY STUDIO
ADAPTED BY EYVIND EARLE

gb GOLDEN PRESS
Western Publishing Company, Inc.
Racine, Wisconsin

This Little Golden Book was produced under the supervision of

THE WALT DISNEY STUDIO

Fifteenth Printing, 1976

Once upon a time there were three children, Wendy, John, and Michael Darling by name.

They liked bedtime, because every night in the
nursery Wendy told stories about Peter Pan.
Peter is a little boy who decided never to grow up.

He lives in a far-away
Never Land, full of adventure and fun.

The children loved to hear stories about him. And Peter Pan himself (with the fairy, Tinker Bell) would come flying down and sit on the nursery window sill to hear the stories. One night Peter asked the children to come with him to the Never Land.

Wendy was delighted. And Peter taught them how to fly—it was as easy as one, two, three. All it took was a wish and pinch of pixie dust—and a little practice, too.

Then out the nursery window they flew, and
away to the Never Land.

The Never Land was a wonderful place—an
island in a nameless sea.

There were fairies living in the treetops.
There were mermaids swimming in a lagoon.
There were real red Indians in a village on a cliff.
There were woods full of wild animals.

Best of all, there was a shipful of pirates—wicked ones, with a specially wicked leader, Captain Hook.

Wendy, John, and Michael knew at first sight that they would love the Never Land. And they did.

They liked Peter's wonderful underground house, with lots of hidden doorways in a great big hollow tree. There they met the Lost Boys who shared Peter's home. And the Boys were delighted that Wendy had come to tell bedtime stories to them.

But they did not spend much time in that underground house. There were too many exciting things to do.

Sometimes they played at war with the red Indians, who were really their very good friends.

Sometimes they had trouble with the wicked pirates, who were their enemies.

One day the pirates stole away Princess Tiger Lily of the Indian tribe.

The Indian Chief, her father, was all upset. But Peter Pan rescued Tiger Lily and brought her safely home again.

That made Captain Hook, the leader of the pirates, madder at Peter Pan than he had ever been.

"I'll catch that Pan if it's the last thing I do!" he vowed. And he laid a wicked plan.

He kidnapped Wendy, John, and Michael and all the Lost Boys while Peter was away. And he took them to his pirate ship.

"Now, my fine fellows," said Captain Hook, when he had the Boys and Wendy on his ship, "which will it be? Will you all turn pirates, or do you want to walk the plank, and fall *kerplash* into the sea?"

"I guess we'll turn pirates," said the Boys.
But Wendy would have none of that.
"I think you should be ashamed of yourselves,"
she said. "Peter Pan will rescue us."

And she was right. For at the last minute Peter Pan appeared.

He beat Captain Hook in a good, fair fight, and he freed every one of his friends. They scared those bad pirates into jumping overboard and rowing away in their boat.

"Hurrah!" cried Pan. "Now the pirate ship is ours!"

"Where shall we sail to?" cried the Boys.

"It's time we went home," Wendy said.

"If you must go home, we'll sail there," said Peter Pan.

With a wish and a pinch of pixie dust, they made that pirate ship fly! And away they all sailed on that ship, through the sky, to the nursery window again.

The children's parents could scarcely believe that their children had been to the Never Land. But Wendy, John, and Michael, even when they grew up, never forgot Peter Pan.